Kingcup Cottage

written and illustrated by Racey Helps

" Whenever choosing a house," Old Uncle Frog used to say,

" see that there are plenty of damp patches on the walls —

and if the roof leaks, so much the better."

When she had to find a home of her own Francesca remembered

his words. She rented

KINGCUP COTTAGE.

Kingcup Cottage would have pleased Old
Uncle Frog. It sagged oosily among
tree roots at the edge of Heron
Lake.

Snails loved it.

And here Francesca lived happily enough among the marsh marigolds.
" I have water laid on in every room," she would say,
" so what more could I want ? "

Yet sometimes she felt a trifle lonely.
Apart from snails she saw nobody —
and snails were not talkative.
Whenever she said " Good-morning "
they popped back into
their shells.

Now, as everybody knows, the best way to get to know people is to hold a PARTY.

So it was that just before her birthday Francesca sat down and wrote out a big pile of INVITATION CARDS. The ink ran a little on the damp paper. Mr. Dragonfly, who was the Lake Postman, delivered the invitations to all the best nests and burrows in the district.

In some of these houses lived

people who could not read.

Several thought the invitation

was a letter from the landlord

asking for the rent. It made

them very unhappy. Mr. Bun

was quite bad-tempered all day!

" I'm sure it *looks* like a summons," thought
Mr. Mole. He decided to begin his long winter sleep very
early this year. Several people found the invitation cards, when
dried out, made useful draught stoppers.

The DAY OF THE PARTY came.

Francesca got up extra early in order to make the cakes and jellies in good time.

The flour in the bags seemed to be dough already, and as there was a shortage of currants she dipped into her supply of dried flies.

No expense was spared.

At last everything was ready and Francesca sat down
to await her guests. She waited — and waited.
Nobody arrived. Afternoon wore into
evening and still there wasn't
a single guest!

The jellies slowly
turned into pink and green water.

Francesca ate one of her cakes.

"I think I should have put in more flies,"
she told herself.

Then she pulled a cracker
and put on a funny hat and had some
jelly through a straw.

But it wasn't much fun.

When she got up the following morning
and saw the unused plates her feelings overcame her.
She felt she could not bear to look at them, so she went to the
far side of the lake for a quiet cry. It was here that
Pinny Needlekin came upon her.

Pinny had come to the lake looking for
While sailing it the day before he had tu
Now he went up to Francesca and poked
his nos

eyes ar
" Perh

He *hate*
— esp
if it wa
e
H

ost boat.

led into the water and lost it.

gently with

" Please, Ma'am, do dry your

ell me your trouble " he said.

s I may be able to help you."

eeing anybody in tears

ally a lady.   He did wonder

ossible to dry eyes or anything

with such a soggy hanky.

elt sure it   would probably

" dry them wetter."

Between sniffs Francesca
croaked out her trouble.

Pinny, who had received one of the
invitation cards, felt cross with
himself

— he had used it to make a sail for a boat!

" — and after all my trouble
n–nobody c–came at all! " ended Francesca.
Pinny agreed that birthday parties are not much use
without people to
go to them.

He watched the swallows flying low over the lake in the morning mist and asked himself why *he* had not gone to Francesca's party.

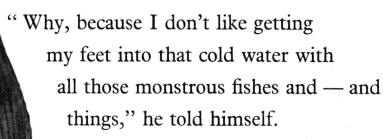

" Why, because I don't like getting my feet into that cold water with all those monstrous fishes and — and things," he told himself.

" Besides, too much damp gives me cramp in the toes."

From out of the mist came the harsh cry of a heron and Francesca hopped away and poked herself in among the forget-me-nots.

" I think I know why nobody went to your nice party, ma'am," said Pinny, following her. " It was because your house is too watery. I'm sure it's a very nice house," he went on quickly, " but so many folk don't like getting wet, you know. They catch cold, or big fish catch *them* — and some can't swim! "

" Not like getting wet! " croaked Francesca in amazement. " Really ?
I had not thought of that." All trace of woe left her face. She
knew Pinny was right. Damp places were all right for frogs and
snails but some people just did not care for them at all.

" I shall have a SECOND PARTY! " she cried, clapping her hands.
" I will start preparing for it now — and I'll hold it high above
the water in Toadstool Dell." She would have kissed Pinny, only
his prickles looked a little sharp.

Next moment there was a splash
and Francesca disappeared.

Pinny waited on the
shore until the kingcups round the
cottage began to quiver ; then he
knew she had reached home.

" I'm glad there's going
to be another party after all," he nodded.
" I wonder if there will be worm sandwiches. . . ."

The following morning Mr. Dragonfly was delivering invitation cards once again — and this time he took a little longer over it as Francesca insisted he should *read aloud* each card as it was delivered.

Mr. Mole, already snoring gently in his little bed, refused to wake up.

No-one ever saw such a bustle and scurry
as there was in the kitchen of Kingcup Cottage
on the day of the Second Party.

And what a coming and going
there was later as Francesca took her good things
to the shore on her lily-leaf boat!

Luckily ducks and herons
seem to have been busy elsewhere
that day!

And what a difference *this* party was! Almost everybody came. The mole did not, neither did Mr. Dragonfly, who had lost his voice and declared he was " sick of parties."

As Pinny had been thoughtful enough to place a few notices here and there to direct people to Toadstool Dell few guests got lost on the way

. . . just a couple who could not read anyway, but who managed

to find the party before all the fun was over.

As for the party itself, well, you can see what a success
it was! Everybody enjoyed it, even though the jellies *did* taste
a little of tadpole ; and Francesca's party was to be talked of for many
a long day to come. As Pinny said, " I should like to go
to a party like that every day
— and *twice* on Sundays! "

Francesca is now looking for rooms
where she can have her less damp friends
in for afternoon tea. If you do happen to know
of some perhaps you will tell her; but on no
account, she says, must the rooms be

puddly.

The End